The Beaver ~~~~ ~~ Revolting Rhymes

Whether they're about eating fleas, worms or eels, disgusting habits, gruesome details of death and destruction, or even insulting things to say to people, the poems in this book really are revolting! They will appeal to your worst possible sense of humour – and it is not advisable to read them at mealtimes!

Jennifer Curry has written lots of books for children; *Treasure Trove* and *The Beaver Book of Skool Verse* are her other Beaver titles. Graeme Curry, her son, is a singer and writer and lives in Oxford.

The Beaver Book of REVOLTING RHYMES

Jennifer and Graeme Curry

Illustrated by David Mostyn

Beaver Books

First published in 1983 by
The Hamlyn Publishing Group Limited
London · New York · Sydney · Toronto
Astronaut House, Feltham, Middlesex, England

© Copyright this collection Jennifer and Graeme Curry 1983
© Copyright illustrations the Hamlyn Publishing Group Limited 1983
ISBN 0 600 20670 X

Printed and bound in Great Britain by
Cox & Wyman Limited, Reading
Set in Baskerville

To Roger, with friendship and thanks

Contents

Introduction

Don't Cry Darling, It's Blood All Right

Whenever poets want to give you the idea that
 something is particularly meek and mild,
They compare it to a child,
Thereby proving that though poets with poetry may
 be rife
They don't know the facts of life.
If of compassion you desire either a tittle or a jot,
Don't try to get it from a tot.
Hard-boiled, sophisticated adults like me and you
May enjoy ourselves thoroughly with *Little Women*
 and *Winnie-the-Pooh*,
But innocent infants these titles from their reading
 course eliminate
As soon as they discover that it was honey and nuts
 and mashed potatoes instead of human flesh that
 Winnie-the-Pooh and Little Women ate.
Innocent children have no use for fables about
 rabbits or donkeys or tortoises or porpoises,
What they want is something with plenty of well-
 mutilated corpoises.
Not on legends of how the rose came to be a rose
 instead of a petunia is their fancy fed,
But on the inside story of how somebody's bones got
 ground up to make somebody else's bread.
They'll go to sleep listening to the story of the little
 beggarmaid who got to be queen by being kind to
 the bees and the birds,
But they're all eyes and ears the minute they suspect
 a wolf or a giant is going to tear some poor
 woodcutter into quarters or thirds.

It doesn't take much to fill their cup;
All they want is for somebody to be eaten up.
Therefore I say unto you, all you poets who are so
crazy about meek and mild little children and their
angelic air,
If you are sincere and really want to please them,
why not just go out and get yourselves devoured by
a bear.

Ogden Nash

Foul Food

Worm Song

Nobody loves me, everybody hates me,
Just 'cos I eat worms,
Long thin slimy ones, short fat hairy ones,
Ooosy gooey oosy gooey worms.

Long thin slimy ones slip down easily,
The short fat hairy ones stick,
Short fat hairy ones stick in your teeth,
And the juice goes squelch like this.

You bite off their heads and suck out the juice,
And you throw the skins away,
Nobody knows how I survive
On a hundred worms a day.

Two Sad

It's such a shock, I almost screech,
When I find a worm inside my peach!
But then, what really makes me blue
Is to find a worm who's bit in two!

William Cole

Grace

For what we have put back on the dish
May the school chickens be truly grateful.

School Dinners

What's for dinner? What's for dinner?
Irish spew, Irish spew,
Sloppy semolina, sloppy semolina,
No thank you, no thank you.

Splishy splashy custard, dead dogs' eyes,
All mixed up with giblet pies,
Spread it on the butty nice and thick,
Swallow it down with a bucket of sick.

Hotch scotch, bogie pie,
Mix it up with a dead man's eye
Hard-boiled snails, slapped on thick,
Wash it down with a cup of cold sick.

Mister Kelly

Old Mister Kelly
Had a pimple on his belly.
His wife cut it off
And it tasted just like jelly.

Grannie Caught a Flea

A B C
My Grannie caught a flea
She salted it, and peppered it,
And had it for her tea.

One Two Three

One two three
    Father caught a flea.
Put him in the teapot
    To make a cup of tea.

The Eel

I don't mind eels
Except as meals.
And the way they feels.

Ogden Nash

Eels

Eileen Carroll
Had a barrel
Filled with writhing eels
And just for fun
She swallowed one:
Now she knows how it feels.

Spike Milligan

Deedle Deedle Dumpling, My Son John

Deedle deedle dumpling, my son John,
Ate a pasty five feet long;
He bit it once, he bit it twice,
Oh, my goodness, it was full of mice!

The Sleepy Giant

My age is three hundred and seventy-two,
    And I think, with the deepest regret,
How I used to pick up and voraciously chew
    The dear little boys whom I met.

I've eaten them raw, in their holiday suits;
    I've eaten them curried with rice;
I've eaten them baked, in their jackets and boots,
    And found them exceedingly nice.

But now that my jaws are too weak for such fare,
    I think it exceedingly rude
To do such a thing, when I'm quite well aware
    Little boys do not like to be chewed.

And so I contentedly live upon eels,
    And try to do nothing amiss,
And I pass all the time I can spare from my meals
    In innocent slumber – like this.

Charles Edward Carryl

The Witch's Work Song

Two spoons of sherry,
Three ounces of yeast,
Half a pound of unicorn,
And God bless the feast.
Shake them in the colander,
Bang them to a chop,
Simmer slightly, snip up nicely,
Jump, skip, hop.
Knit one, knot one, purl two together,
Pip one and pop one and pluck the secret feather.
Baste in a mod. oven.
God bless our coven.
Tra-la-la!
Three toads in a jar.
Te-he-he!
Put in the frog's knee.
Peep out of the lace curtain.
There goes the Toplady girl, she's up to no good
    that's certain.
Oh, what a lovely baby!
How nice it would go with gravy.
Pinch the salt,
Turn the malt
With a hey-nonny-nonny and I don't mean maybe.

T. H. White

Some Soupy Limericks

'Waiter! This soup has a smell
Reminiscent of brimstone from hell.
  The taste is as foul
   As a decomposed owl,
And it looks like the slime on a well.'

There was an old farmer from Slough
Who always drank soup on his plough.
  When asked why this was,
   He said, 'It's because
My wife says I make such a row.'

A cannibal once asked his guest
What missionary soup he liked best.
  Said the guest: 'Fear no waste,
   I have Catholic taste,
But a Protestant's fine, if you're pressed.'

There was a young fellow called Fred
Who liked to drink soup while in bed.
   But one day it spilt
   All over his quilt
So he ate all his bedclothes instead.

Stephen Rhys Brown

Wilhelmina Mergenthaler

Wilhelmina Mergenthaler
Had a lovely ermine collar
Made of just the nicest fur,
That her mamma bought for her.
Once, when mamma was away,
Out a-shopping for the day,
   Wilhelmina Mergenthaler
   Ate her lovely ermine collar.

Harry P. Taber

An Old Man From Peru

There was an old man from Peru
Who dreamt he was eating his shoe.
   He awoke in the night
   In a terrible fright
And found it was perfectly true.

Telly-pie-tit

Telly-pie-tit
Sat upon a wall
Eating raw cabbages,
Slugs, snails and all.

Children's playground rhyme

18

A Thousand Hairy Savages

A thousand hairy savages
Sitting down to lunch
Gobble gobble glup glup
Munch munch munch.

Spike Milligan

The Melancholy Cannibal

Roly-poly Herbert Hannibal
Met a melancholy cannibal.
Said the cannibal: 'Nice to meet you,
But I'm afraid I *cannot* eat you.'
And then he added, somewhat flustered,
'You see, I've just run out of custard!'

Colin West

Mustard

I'm mad about mustard –
Even on custard.

Ogden Nash

The Centipede's Song

'I've eaten many strange and scrumptious dishes in
    my time,
Like jellied gnats and dandyprats and earwigs
    cooked in slime,
And mice with rice – they're really nice
When roasted in their prime.
(But don't forget to sprinkle them with just a pinch of
    grime.)

'I've eaten fresh mudburgers by the greatest cooks
    there are,
And scrambled dregs and stinkbugs' eggs and
    hornets stewed in tar,
And pails of snails and lizards' tails,
And beetles by the jar.
(A beetle is improved by just a splash of vinegar.)

'I often eat boiled slobbages. They're grand when
    served beside
Minced doodlebugs and curried slugs. And have you
    ever tried
Mosquitoes' toes and wampfish roes
Most delicately fried?
(The only trouble is they disagree with my inside.)

'I'm mad for crispy wasp-stings on a piece of
    buttered toast,
And pickled spines of porcupines. And then a
    gorgeous roast
Of dragon's flesh, well hung, not fresh
It costs a pound at most,
(And comes to you in barrels if you order it by post.)

'I crave the tasty tentacles of octopi for tea
I like hot-dogs, I *love* hot-frogs, and surely you'll
   agree
A plate of soil with engine oil's
A super recipe.
(I hardly need to mention that it's practically free.)

'For dinner on my birthday shall I tell you what I
   chose:
Hot noodles made from poodles on a slice of garden
   hose –
And a rather smelly jelly
Made of armadillo's toes.
(The jelly is delicious, but you have to hold your
   nose.)

'Now comes,' the Centipede declared, 'the burden of
   my speech:
These foods are rare beyond compare – some are
   right out of reach;
But there's no doubt I'd go without
A million plates of each
For one small mite,
One tiny bite
Of this FANTASTIC PEACH!'

Roald Dahl

The Boy Stood in the Supper-room

The boy stood in the supper-room
   Whence all but he had fled;
He'd eaten seven pots of jam
   And he was gorged with bread.

'Oh, one more crust before I bust!'
   He cried in accents wild;
He licked the plates, he sucked the spoons—
   He was a vulgar child.

There came a burst of thunder-sound—
   The boy – oh! where was he?
Ask of the maid who mopped him up,
   The breadcrumbs and the tea!

Anon.

Happy Birthday To You!

Happy birthday to you!
Squashed tomatoes and stew;
Bread and butter in the gutter,
Happy birthday to you!

Children's playground song

Henry King

The Chief Defect of Henry King
Was chewing little bits of String.
At last he swallowed some which tied
Itself in ugly Knots inside.
Physicians of the Utmost Fame
Were called at once; but when they came
They answered, as they took their Fees,
'There is no Cure for this Disease.
Henry will very soon be dead.'
His parents stood about his Bed
Lamenting his Untimely Death,
When Henry, with his Latest Breath
Cried, 'Oh, my Friends, be warned by me,
That Breakfast, Dinner, Lunch and Tea
Are all the Human Frame requires . . .'
With that, the Wretched Child expires.

Hilaire Belloc

Little Lord William

Little Lord William was the son of a gourmet,
Only the choicest foods entered his tourmet,
But he liked nothing more, after wolfing his snails,
Than to eat a large bowl of fresh fingernails.

Little Lord William enjoyed avocado,
And ate six more courses, all with bravado,
But he liked nothing more, after aspic and quails,
Than to eat a large bowl of fresh fingernails.

Little Lord William took a glass of champagne,
Dabbed at his lips and began eating again,
But he liked nothing more, after oysters in pails,
Than to eat a large bowl of fresh fingernails.

Little Lord William ate candied peel,
The perfect end to the perfect meal,
But he like nothing more, after jellied oxtails,
Than to eat a large bowl of fresh fingernails.

Graeme Curry

Good King Arthur

When good King Arthur ruled this land,
    He was a goodly king;
He stole three pecks of barley-meal,
    To make a bag-pudding.

A bag-pudding the king did make,
    And stuff'd it well with plums;
And in it put great lumps of fat,
    As big as my two thumbs.

The king and queen did eat thereof,
    And noblemen beside;
And what they could not eat that night,
    The queen next morning fried.

Anon.

Frankly Physical

Mister Fatty Belly

Mister Fatty Belly, how is your wife?
Very ill, very ill, up all night,
Can't eat a bit of fish
Nor a bit of liquorice.
O-U-T spells 'out' and out you must go
With a jolly good clout on your ear-hole spout.

Mother Made a Seedy Cake

Mother made a seedy cake,
Gave us all the belly ache;
Father bought a pint of beer,
Gave us all the diarrhoea.

Oh My Finger, Oh My Thumb

Oh my finger, oh my thumb,
Oh my belly, oh my bum.

Children's playground games

Amelia

Amelia mixed the mustard,
  She mixed it good and thick;
She put it in the custard
  And made her Mother sick,
And showing satisfaction
  By many a loud hurrah,
'Observe,' she said, 'the action
  Of mustard on Mamma'.

A. E. Housman

Twickenham

There was a young lady of Twickenham,
Whose boots were too tight to walk quickenham.
  She bore them awhile,
  But at last, at a stile,
She pulled them both off and was sickenham.

A Young Lady of Spain

There was a young lady of Spain
Who was dreadfully sick on a train,
    Not once, but again
    And again and again,
And again and again and again.

Quick, Quick, the Cat's Been Sick

Quick, quick,
The cat's been sick.

Where? Where?
Under the chair.

Hasten, hasten,
Fetch the basin.

No, no,
Fetch the po.

Kate, Kate, you're far too late,
The carpet's in a dreadful state.

Children's playground song

A Riddle

Because I am by nature blind,
I wisely choose to walk behind;
However, to avoid disgrace,
I let no creature see my face.
My words are few, but spoke with sense:
And yet my speaking gives offence:
Or, if to whisper I presume,
The company will fly the room.
By all the world I am oppressed,
But my oppression gives them rest.

Jonathan Swift

Answer: Bum

Beans

Beans, beans, they're good for the heart,
The more you eat, the more you fart,
The more you fart, the better you feel,
So let's have beans with every meal.

A Student from Sparta

A musical student from Sparta
Was a truly magnificent farter;
   On the strength of one bean
   He'd fart 'God Save The Queen',
And Beethoven's *Moonlight Sonata*.

Inky Pinky

Inky pinky, pen and inky,
I smell a dirty stinky.

Children's playground rhyme

Papa Moses Killed a Skunk

Papa Moses killed a skunk
Mama Moses cooked the skunk
Baby Moses ate the skunk
My oh my oh how they stunk.

Traditional American rhyme

Under the Apple Tree

As I sat under the apple tree,
A birdie sent his love to me,
And as I wiped it from my eye,
I said, 'Thank goodness, cows can't fly.'

The Black Cat and the White Cat

Oh! the black cat piddled in the white cat's eye,
The white cat said, 'Cor blimey!
'I'm sorry, sir, I piddled in your eye,
I didn't know you was behind me.'

There Was an Old Man from Darjeeling

There was an old man from Darjeeling,
Who boarded a bus bound for Ealing.
    He saw on the door:
    'Please don't spit on the floor,'
So he stood up and spat on the ceiling.

The Story of Little Suck-a-thumb

One day Mamma said, 'Conrad dear
I must go out and leave you here.
But mind now, Conrad, what I say,
Don't suck your thumb while I'm away.
The great tall tailor always comes
To little boys who suck their thumbs;
And ere they dream what he's about,
He takes his great sharp scissors out,
And cuts their thumbs clean off – and then,
You know, they never grow again.'

Mamma had scarcely turned her back,
The thumb was in, Alack! Alack!

The door flew open, in he ran,
The great, long, red-legged scissor-man.
Oh! children, see! the tailor's come
And caught out little Suck-a-Thumb.
Snip! Snap! Snip! the scissors go;
And Conrad cries out, 'Oh! Oh! Oh!'
Snip! Snap! Snip! They go so fast,
That both his thumbs are off at last.

Mamma comes home: there Conrad stands,
And looks quite sad, and shows his hands;
'Ah!' said Mamma, 'I knew he'd come
To naughty little Suck-a-Thumb.'

Heinrich Hoffman

The Sniffle

In spite of her sniffle,
Isabel's chiffle.
Some girls with a sniffle
Would be weepy and tiffle;
They would look awful,
Like a rained-on waffle,
But Isabel's chiffle
In spite of her sniffle.
Her nose is more red
With a cold in her head,
But then, to be sure,
Her eyes are bluer.
Some girls with a snuffle,
Their tempers are uffle,
But when Isabel's snivelly
She's snivelly civilly,
And when she's snuffly
She's perfectly luffly.

Ogden Nash

My Nose

It doesn't breathe; it doesn't smell;
It doesn't feel so very well.
I am disgusted with my nose.
The only thing it does is blows.

The Boy Stood on the Burning Deck

The boy stood on the burning deck
Picking his nose like mad;
He rolled them into little balls
And flicked them at his dad.

Nasty Habit

Pick it
Lick it
Roll it
Flick it.

Don't Poke Your Nose

Mind your own business,
Fry your own fish,
Don't poke your nose
Into my clean dish.

Children's playground rhymes

Teeth

English Teeth, English Teeth!
Shining in the sun
A part of British heritage
Aye, each and every one.

English Teeth, Happy Teeth!
Always having fun
Clamping down on bits of fish
And sausages half done.

English Teeth! HEROES' Teeth!
Hear them click! and clack!
Let's sing a song of praise to them—
Three Cheers for the Brown Grey and Black.

Spike Milligan

Say 'Aagh!'

No fun being the dentist.
  Not much fun as a job:
Spending all of your days in gazing
  Right into everyone's gob.

No fun *seeing* the dentist.
  Not much fun at all:
Staring straight up his hairy nostrils—
  Drives you up the wall!

Kit Wright

After the Ball

After the ball was over
She lay on the sofa and sighed.
She put her false teeth in salt water
And took out her lovely glass eye.
She kicked her cork leg in the corner
And hung up her wig on the wall,
The rest of her went to bye-byes,
After the ball.

Children's playground song

Ermyntrude

A little girl named Ermyntrude
Was often curiously rude—
Came down to breakfast in the nude.
Her sister said (though not a prude):
'It seems to me extremely crude
To see your tummy over food:
Your conduct borders on the lewd.
Also, you nastily exude
Cornflakes and milk as though you'd spewed.'—
Her lips were open when she chewed,
And read a comic book called *Dude*.
She was a sight not to be viewed
Without profound disquietude.
Though what could come but such a mood
From anyone named Ermyntrude?

Roy Fuller

A Close Thing

Smith Minor, whose first name was Paul,
Just narrowly missed a bad fall—
He broke several teeth
And the jawbone beneath,
Seven ribs, and a leg, but that's all!

Sam, Sam

Sam, Sam, the dirty man,
Washed his face in a frying pan;
He combed his hair with a donkey's tail,
And scratched his belly with a big toenail.

Children's playground rhyme

from Melodies

There was once a young man of Oporta
Who daily got shorter and shorter,
    The reason he said
    Was the hod on his head,
Which was filled with the *heaviest* mortar.

His sister named Lucy O'Finner,
Grew constantly thinner and thinner,
    The reason was plain,
    She slept out in the rain,
And was never allowed any dinner.

Lewis Carroll

Grim, Gruesome and Ghoulish

All, All A-Lonely

Three little children sitting on the sand,
All, all a-lonely,
Three little children sitting on the sand,
All, all a-lonely,
Down in the green wood shady—
There came an old woman, said, 'Come on with me,'
All, all a-lonely,
There came an old woman, said, 'Come on with me,'
All, all a-lonely,
Down in the green wood shady—
She stuck her penknife through their heart,
All, all a-lonely,
She stuck her penknife through their heart,
All, all a-lonely,
Down in the green wood shady.

Anon.

A Little Boy Threw

It snowed a mist, it snowed a mist,
It snowed all over the land:
Till all the boys throughout the town
Went out with ball in hand.

A little boy threw his ball so high,
He threw his ball so low;
He threw it into a dusky garden
Among the blades of snow.

'Come here, come here, you sweet little boy,
Come here and get your ball.'
'I'll not come here and I'll not come there,
And I'll not come in your hall.'

She showed him an apple as yellow as gold,
She showed him a bright gold ring,
She showed him a cherry as red as blood,
And that enticed him in;

Enticed him into the sitting-room,
Enticed him into the kitchen,
And there he saw his own dear nurse
A-picking of a chicken.

'I'm washing this basin the livelong day,
To catch your heart's blood in;
And I won't spare you nor yet your ma,
Nor any of your kin.'

And she dragged him to the cooling board,
And stabbed him like a sheep,
And threw him into the dusky well,
With his grammar at his feet.

Anon.

Skin and Bone

There was a woman all skin and bone
Who lived in a cottage all on her own,
   Oo-oo-oo!

She thought she'd go to church one day
To hear the parson preach and pray,
   Oo-oo-oo!

When she got to the wooden stile
She thought she'd stay and rest a while.
   Oo-oo-oo!

When she reached the old church door
A ghastly ghost lay on the floor,
   Oo-oo-oo!

The grubs crawled in, the grubs crawled out
Of its ears, nose and mouth.
   Oo-oo-oo!

'Oh you ghastly ghost,' she said,
'Shall I be like you when I am dead?'
   Ye-ee-es!

Children's playground rhyme

Sally Simpkin's Lament

'Oh! what is that comes gliding in,
    And quite in middling haste?
It is the picture of my Jones,
    And painted to the waist.

It is not painted to the life,
    For where's the trousers blue?
Oh, Jones, my dear! – Oh dear! my Jones,
    What is become of you?'

'Oh! Sally dear, it is too true,—
    The half that you remark
Is come to say my other half
    Is bit off by a shark!

Oh! Sally, sharks do things by halves,
    Yet most completely do!
A bite in one place seems enough,
    But I've been bit in two.

You know I once was all your own,
　　But now a shark must share!
But let that pass – for now to you
　　I'm neither here nor there.

Alas! death has a strange divorce
　　Effected in the sea,
It has divided me from you,
　　And even me from me.

Don't fear my ghost will walk o' nights,
　　To haunt as people say;
My ghost *can't* walk, for oh! my legs
　　Are many leagues away!

Lord! think when I am swimming round,
　　And looking where the boat is,
A shark just snaps away a half
　　Without a quarter's notice.

One half is here, the other half
　　Is near Columbia placed:
Oh! Sally, I have got the whole
　　Atlantic for my waist.

But now adieu – a long adieu!
　　I've solved death's awful riddle,
And would say more, but I am doomed
　　To break off in the middle.'

Thomas Hood

The Knee On Its Own

A lone knee wanders through the world,
    A knee and nothing more;
It's not a tent, it's not a tree,
    A knee and nothing more.

In battle once there was a man
    Shot foully through and through;
The knee alone remained unhurt
    As saints are said to do.

Since then it's wandered through the world,
    A knee and nothing more.
It's not a tent, it's not a tree,
    A knee and nothing more.

Christian Morgenstern
(translated by R. F. C. Hull)

Mary's Ghost

'Twas in the middle of the night,
    To sleep young William tried;
When Mary's ghost came stealing in,
    And stood at his bed-side.

O William dear! O William dear!
    My rest eternal ceases;
Alas! my everlasting peace
    Is broken into pieces.

The body-snatchers they have come,
   And made a snatch at me;
It's very hard them kind of men
   Won't let a body be!

The arm that used to take your arm
   Is took to Dr Vyse;
And both my legs are gone to walk
   The hospital at Guy's.

I vowed that you should have my hand
   But fate gives us denial;
You'll find it there, at Dr Bell's,
In spirits and a phial.

As for my feet, the little feet
   You used to call so pretty,
There's one, I know, in Bedford Row,
   The t'other's in the City.

I can't tell where my head is gone,
   But Dr Carpue can;
As for my trunk, it's all packed up
   To go by Pickford's van.

The cock it crows – I must be gone!
   My William, we must part!
But I'll be yours in death, although
   Sir Astley has my heart.

Don't go to weep upon my grave,
   And think that there I be;
They haven't left an atom there
   Of my anatomie.

Thomas Hood

Mother Knows Best

I've lots of pets, some small, some big—
a cat, a rabbit, a guinea-pig,
a budgie, dear to all of us
and Oliver, my octopus.
Oliver's a bit of a freak
he has two huge eyes, a parrot beak,
a jelly-bag belly,
shaped like a gong
and eight rubber arms, each three feet long.
Mum says Oliver's dangerous.
Well, you know what mums are. Ridiculous.
How can Oliver, gentle and dumb,
climb out of his aquarium?

Mystery of mysteries, one day
Belle the budgie flew away.
Two days later, just as weird,
Gilbert the guinea-pig disappeared.

I fed my pets next day – good habit—
but where was Reginald, my rabbit?
Caroline, my tortoiseshell cat
had gone the morning after that.

Mum cried, for Mum was fond of her,
when Oliver began to purr.
I went to bed at ten to nine,
sobbing for dear friends of mine—
Belle, Gilbert, Reginald, Caroline.
I'd nearly cried myself to sleep
when I heard something or someone creep
very quietly, on all four pairs
of plop, plop, plop, plop feet upstairs.
My hair and I stood up with fright.
My heart went mad.
Oh, was I glad
I'd locked my bedroom door that night.
Maybe, after all, Mum was right.

R. C. Scriven

The Slithergadee

The Slithergadee has crawled out of the sea,
He may catch all the others, but he won't catch me.
No you won't catch me, old Slithergadee,
You may catch all the others, but you wo—

Shel Silverstein

The Wendigo

The Wendigo,
The Wendigo!
Its eyes are ice and indigo!
Its blood is rank and yellowish!
Its voice is hoarse and bellowish!
Its tentacles are slithery,
And scummy,
Slimy,
Leathery!
Its lips are hungry blubbery,
And smacky,
Sucky,
Rubbery!

The Wendigo,
The Wendigo!
I saw it just a friend ago!
Last night it lurked in Canada;
Tonight, on your veranada!
As you are lolling hammockwise
It contemplates you stomachwise.
You loll,
It contemplates,
It lollops.
The rest is merely gulps and gollops.

Ogden Nash

The Swank

The Swank is quick and full of vice,
He tortures beetles also mice.
He bites their legs off and he beats them
Into a pulp, and then he eats them.

V. C. Vickers

The Boa Constrictor

I'm being swallowed by a boa constrictor, a boa
   constrictor, a boa constrictor,
I'm being swallowed by a boa constrictor,
And I don't like it one bit.

Oh no! It's up to my toe.
Oh gee! It's up to my knee.
Oh fiddle! It's up to my middle.
Oh heck! It's up to my neck.
Oh dread! It's up to my . . . GULP.

Shel Silverstein

Dragon Poem

He comes in the night, killing all greenery,
with his spikey tail and rough scabby skin
killing all the humans and spitting the bones
   in the bin.

Frances Edwards (aged 11)

The Demon Manchanda

The two-headed two-body,
the Demon Manchanda
had eyes bigger than his belly.
He walked and talked
right round the world
but every time he opened his mouth
he put his foot in it.

'You're pulling my leg,'
he said to himself.
So he ate his words instead.
I suppose you know the rest:
he went to the window
and threw out his chest.

Michael Rosen

The Hens From Never-when

The angry hens from Never-when
had a fight and lost their legs.
Now it's hot
where they squat
and they're laying soft-boiled eggs.

Michael Rosen

The Long, Long Worm

There's a long, long worm a-crawling
Across the roof of my tent.
I can hear the whistle calling,
And it's time that I went.
There's the cold, cold water waiting
For me to take my morning dip.
And when I come back I'll find that worm
Upon my pillowslip.

Children's playground song

In the Bathroom

What is that blood-stained thing—
Hairy, as if it were frayed—
Stretching itself along
The slippery bath's steep side?

I approach it, ready to kill,
Or run away, aghast;
And find I have to deal
With a used elastoplast.

Roy Fuller

The Germ

A mighty creature is the germ,
Though smaller than the pachyderm.
His customary dwelling place
Is deep within the human race.
His childish pride he often pleases
By giving people strange diseases.
Do you, my poppet, feel infirm?
You probably contain a germ.

Ogden Nash

The Happy Family

Before the children say goodnight,
  Mother, Father, stop and think:
Have you screwed their heads on tight?
  Have you washed their ears with ink?

Have you said and done and thought
  All that earnest parents should?
Have you beat them as you ought:
  Have you begged them to be good?

And above all – when you start
  Out the door and douse the light—
Think, be certain, search your heart:
  Have you screwed their heads on tight?

If they sneeze when they're asleep,
  Will their little heads come off?
If they just breathe very deep?
  If – especially – they cough?

Should – alas! – the little dears
  Lose a little head or two,
Have you inked their little ears:
  Girls' ears pink and boys' ears blue?

Children's heads are very loose.
  Mother, Father, screw them tight.
If you feel uncertain use
  A monkey wrench, but do it right.

If a head should come unscrewed
  You will know that you have failed.
Doubtful cases should be glued.
  Stubborn cases should be nailed.

Then when all your darlings go
    Sweetly screaming off to bed,
Mother, Father, you may know
    Angels guard each little head.

Come the morning you will find
    One by one each little head
Full of gentle thoughts and kind,
    Sweetly screaming to be fed.

John Ciardi

Death and Destruction

Notting Hill Polka

We've – had—
A Body in the house
   Since Father passed away;
He took bad on
Saturday night an' he
   Went the followin' day.

Mum's – pulled—
The blinds all down
   An' bought some Sherry Wine,
An' we've put the tin
What the Arsenic's in
   At the bottom of the Ser-pen-tine!

W. Bridges-Adams

Sister Nell

In the family drinking well
Willie pushed his sister Nell.
She's there yet, because it kilt her—
Now we have to buy a filter.

Quiet Fun

My son Augustus, in the street, one day,
    Was feeling quite exceptionally merry.
A stranger asked him: 'Can you tell me, pray,
    The quickest way to Brompton Cemetery?'
'The quickest way? You bet I can!' said Gus,
    And pushed the fellow underneath a bus.

*   *   *

Whatever people say about my son,
He does enjoy his little bit of fun.

Harry Graham

Sammy Watkins

Young Sammy Watkins jumped out of bed;
He ran to his sister and cut off her head.
This gave his dear mother a great deal of pain;
She hopes that he never will do it again.

God Bless

A little boy kneels at the foot of the bed
Saying his evening prayers.
'Dear God, please will you tell my mummy
I'm sorry I pushed her downstairs.
And if my auntie's up there with you
Will you please tell her I'm sorry too,
I didn't know that she would die
If I put poison in the pie.
About the man in the bowler hat,
I didn't mean to shoot his cat.
Sister Jane has gone away
All because she wouldn't play,
I weighed her down with great big rocks
And put her in a wooden box
And then I pushed it into the sea.
I don't think she came home to tea.
And God, I'm really awfully sorry
I pushed poor Charlie under a lorry.
So God bless anyone alive,
It's time, I think, I learnt to drive.'

Peter Tinsley (aged 13)

Impetuous Samuel

Sam had spirits naught could check,
    And today, at breakfast, he
Broke his baby sister's neck,
    So he shan't have jam for tea!

Harry Graham

Crocodile or Alligator?

Crocodile or alligator,
Who is who on the equator?
Which one ate up Auntie Norah,
Famous tropical explorer?

Cool she was and calm she kept, I'll
Bet you that repulsive reptile
Had a hard job as he ate her,
Crocodile *or* alligator.

Norah, sister of my mother,
Couldn't tell one from the other,
Had she only read this fable,
Maybe she'd have then been able.

Crocodiles, with jaws shut tightly,
Show their teeth off impolitely,
But alligators aren't so rude,
And seldom let their teeth protrude.

Whether former, whether latter,
To Aunt Norah doesn't matter,
She's at rest inside his tummy,
What a dinner, yummy, yummy!

Colin West

Social Study

While my mother ate her heart out
And my father chewed the chairs
My sister worked in a factory
Calmly degutting pears:

The green pears like spinach
And the yellow pears like sick
She gently disembowelled
With a deft little flick.

She never seemed to worry
Or share the family fears
But thoughts like bees were buzzing
Inside her golden ears:

She jilted a tin-carpenter
And then a labeller's mate
And finally she married
The man who nails the crate.

She had two lovely children
Called Dorothy and Clem—
They're hanging her tomorrow
For calmly degutting them.

Michael Baldwin

Ruthless Rhyme

'There's been an accident!' they said,
'Your servant's cut in half; he's dead!'
'Indeed!' said Mr Jones, 'and please
Send me the half that's got my keys.'

Harry Graham

Some People

You can't tell some people anything.

I told my friend a secret.
'It dies with me,' he said.
Then he dropped dead.

You can't tell some people anything.

Kit Wright

The Cassowary

Once there was a cassowary
On the plains of Timbuctoo
Killed and ate a missionary
Skin and bones and hymn-book too.

English children's rhyme

Hallelujah!

'Hallelujah!' was the only observation
That escaped Lieutenant-Colonel Mary Jane,
When she tumbled off the platform in the station,
And was cut in little pieces by the train.
    Mary Jane, the train is through yer!
    Hallelujah, Hallelujah!
We shall gather up the fragments that remain.

A. E. Housman

Never Let Your Braces Dangle

Never let your braces dangle,
Never let your braces dangle,
Poor old sport, he got caught,
And went right through the mangle;
Went through the mangle he did, by gum,
Came out like linoleum,
Now he sings in kingdom-come,
'Never let your braces dangle, chum.'

Traditional

Story of Reginald

Cousin Reg is a charming boy—
Just like little Lord Fauntleroy.
All day long he sweetly prattles
Of animals, fairies, kings, and battles.

Dear little chap . . . he bores me stiff!
We'll go for a walk to the top of the cliff;
The cliff is steep and it's lonely, too—
What an adventure, Reg, for you.

COUSIN REG WAS A CHARMING BOY,
JUST LIKE LITTLE LORD FAUNTLEROY . . .

Hubert Phillips

Aunt Maud

I had written to Aunt Maud
Who was on a trip abroad,
When I heard she'd died of cramp
Just too late to save the stamp.

Siesta

She went to bed
To doze,
And rose
To find that she was dead—
How, no one knows.

Stevie Smith

Framed in a First-storey Winder

Framed in a first-storey winder of a burnin' buildin'
Appeared: A Yuman Ead!
'Jump into this net, wot we are 'oldin'
And yule be quite orl right!'

But 'ee wouldn't jump . . .

And the flames grew 'igher and 'igher and 'igher.
   (Phew!)

Framed in a second-storey winder of a burnin'
   buildin'
Appeared: A Yuman Ead!
'Jump into this net, wot we are 'oldin'
And yule be quite orl right!'

But 'ee wouldn't jump . . .

And the flames grew 'igher and 'igher and 'igher.
  (Strewth!)

Framed in a third-storey winder of a burnin'
  buildin'
Appeared: A Yuman Ead!
'Jump into this net, wot we are 'oldin'
And yule be quite orl right!
Honest!'

And 'ee jumped . . .

And 'ee broke 'is bloomin' neck!

Anon.

Epitaph

The manner of her death was thus
She was druv over by a bus.

It Was a Cough

It was a cough that carried her off.
It was a coffin they carried her off in.

A Simple Young Fellow Named Hyde

A simple young fellow named Hyde
In a funeral procession was spied.
   When asked, 'Who is dead?'
   He tittered and said,
'I don't know. I just came for the ride.'

Little Willie

Little Willie's dead,
Shove him in a coffin,
'Cos you don't get the chance
Of a funeral often!

Traditional

Whenever You See a Hearse Go By

Whenever you see a hearse go by
Remember, one day *you*'ve got to die.
   Ooh ah, ooh ah,
   How happy we shall be.

They wrap you in a clean white sheet,
And drop your box down thirteen feet.

All goes well for about a week
And then the coffin begins to leak.

Your eyes fall in and your teeth fall out
And maggots play ping-pong on your snout.

Your fingers rot, and so do your toes,
Your brains come tumbling down your nose.

After a while your face turns green
And pus pours out like clotted cream.

The worms go in and the worms come out,
They go in thin and they come out stout.

So when you see a hearse go by,
Remember one day *you*'ve got to die
   Ooh ah, ooh ah,
   How happy we shall be.

Children's playground song

The Hearse Song

The old Grey Hearse goes rolling by,
You don't know whether to laugh or cry;
For you know some day it'll get you too,
And the hearse's next load may consist of you.

They'll take you out, and they'll lower you down,
While men with shovels stand all around;
They'll throw in dirt, and they'll throw in rocks,
And they don't give a damn if they break the box.

And your eyes drop out and your teeth fall in,
And the worms crawl over your mouth and chin;
They invite their friends and their friends' friends too
And you look like hell when they're through with
    you.

Anon.

Why Nobody Pets the Lion at the Zoo

The morning that the world began
The Lion growled a growl at Man.

And I suspect the lion might
(If he'd been closer) have tried a bite.

I think that's as it ought to be
And not as it was taught to me.

I think the Lion has a right
To growl a growl and bite a bite.

And if the Lion bothered Adam,
He should have growled right back at 'im.

The way to treat a Lion right
Is growl for growl and bite for bite.

True, the Lion is better fit
For biting than for being bit.

But if you look him in the eye
You'll find the Lion's rather shy.

He really wants someone to pet him.
The trouble is: his teeth won't let him.

He has a heart of gold beneath
But the Lion just can't trust his teeth.

John Ciardi

I Had a Hippopotamus

I had a hippopotamus; I kept him in a shed
And fed him upon vitamins and vegetable bread;
I made him my companion on many cheery walks,
And had his portrait done by a celebrity in chalks.

His charming eccentricities were known on every side,
The creature's popularity was wonderfully wide;
He frolicked with the Rector in a dozen friendly
    tussles,
Who could not but remark upon his
    hippopotamuscles.

If he should be afflicted by depression or the dumps,
By Hippopotameasles or the hippopotamumps,
I never knew a particle of peace till it was plain
He was hippopotamasticating properly again.

I had a hippopotamus; I loved him as a friend;
But beautiful relationships are bound to have an end;
Time takes, alas! our joys from us and robs us of our
    blisses;
My hippopotamus turned out a hippopotamissus.

My housekeeper regarded him with jaundice in her
    eye;
She did not want a colony of hippopotami;
She borrowed a machine-gun from her soldier-
    nephew Percy,
And showed my hippopotamus no hippopotamercy.

My house now lacks the glamour that the charming
    creature gave,
The garage where I kept him is as silent as the grave;
No longer he displays among the motor-tyres and
    spanners
His hippopotamastery of hippopotamanners.

No longer now he gambols in the orchard in the
    spring;
No longer do I lead him through the village on a
    string;
No longer in the mornings does the neighbourhood
    rejoice
To his hippopotamusically modulated voice.

I had a hippopotamus; but nothing upon earth
Is constant in its happiness or lasting in its mirth;
No joy that life can bring me can be strong enough to
    smother
My sorrow for that might-have-been-a-
    hippopotamother.

Patrick Barrington

Grizzly Bear

If you ever, ever, ever meet a grizzly bear,
You must never, never, never ask him where
He is going,
Or what he is doing;
For if you ever, ever dare
To stop a grizzly bear,
You will never meet another grizzly bear.

Mary Austin

Terrible Tales

A Norrible Tale

A norrible tale I'm going to tell
Of the woeful tragedy which befell
A family that once resided
In the very same thoroughfare as I did;

Indeed it is a norrible tale,
'Twill make your faces all turn pale,
And your cheeks with tears will be overcome,
Tweedle twaddle, tweedle twaddle twum.

The father in the garden went to walk,
And he cut his throat with a piece of chalk;
The mother, at this was so cut-up
She drowned herself in the water-butt.

The eldest sister, on bended knees
Strangled herself with toasted cheese;
The eldest brother, a charming fella,
Blew out his brains with a gingham umbrella.

The innocent infant lying in the cradle,
Shot itself dead with a silver ladle;
And the maid-servant, not knowing what she did,
Strangled herself with the saucepan lid.

The cat sitting down by the kitchen fire,
Chewed up the fender and did expire;
And a fly on the ceiling – this case is the worst 'un—
Blew itself up with spontaneous combustion.

Now this here family of which I've sung,
If they had not died should have all been hung;
For had they ne'er done themselves any wrong
Why, they might have been here to have heard this
    song.

Old English music-hall song

Lord Randal

'O where have you been, Lord Randal, my son?
O where have you been, my handsome young
        man?'—
    'I have been to the wild wood; mother, make my
        bed soon,
    For I'm weary with hunting, and fain would lie
        down.'

'Who gave you your dinner, Lord Randal, my son?
Who gave you your dinner, my handsome young
        man?'—
    'I dined with my sweetheart; mother, make my
        bed soon,
    For I'm weary with hunting, and fain would lie
        down.'

'What had you for dinner, Lord Randal, my son?
What had you for dinner, my handsome young
        man?'—
    'I had eels boiled in broth; mother, make my bed
        soon,
    For I'm weary with hunting, and fain would lie
        down.'

'And where are your bloodhounds, Lord Randal, my
        son?
And where are your bloodhounds, my handsome
        young man?'—
    'O they swelled and they died; mother, make my
        bed soon,
For I'm weary with hunting, and fain would lie
        down.'

'O I fear you are poisoned, Lord Randal, my son!
O I fear you are poisoned, my handsome young
    man!'—
  'O yes! I am poisoned; mother, make my bed soon,
  For I'm sick at the heart, and I fain would lie
    down.'

Anon.

Father's a Drunkard, and Mother is Dead

Out in the gloomy night, sadly I roam,
    I have no Mother dear, no pleasant home;
Nobody cares for me – no one would cry
    Even if poor little Bessie should die.
Barefoot and tired, I've wandered all day,
    Asking for work – but I'm too small they say;
On the damp ground I must now lay my head––
    'Father's a Drunkard, and Mother is dead!'

CHORUS *Mother, oh! why did you leave me alone,*
            With no one to love me, no friends and no home?
            Dark is the night, and the storm rages wild,
            God pity Bessie, the Drunkard's lone child!

We were so happy till Father drank rum,
    Then all our sorrow and trouble begun;
Mother grew paler, and wept every day,
    Baby and I were too hungry to play.
Slowly they faded, and one Summer's night
    Found their dear faces all silent and white;
Then with big tears slowly dropping, I said:
    'Father's a Drunkard, and Mother is dead!'

CHORUS

Oh! if the 'Temp'rance men' only could find
   Poor, wretched Father, and talk very kind—
If they could stop him from drinking – why, then
   I should be so very happy again!
Is it too late? 'men of Temp'rance', please try,
   Or poor little Bessie may soon starve and die.
All the day long I've been begging for bread—
    'Father's a Drunkard, and Mother is dead!'

CHORUS

                   'Stella'
             Victorian parlour song

Snoozing By the Boozer

All day outside the boozer snores
The boozer-keeper's big brown dog
And carefully each boozer-user
Coming to or from the boozer
Steps around the shaggy snoozer
    Dumped there like a log.

It chanced a fellow named de Souza
(An American composer)
Once was passing by the boozer
Humming to himself a Blues. A
Dog-enthuser, this de Souza,
So he halted by the boozer.
With his stick he poked the snoozer.
'Big brown dog,' he said, 'say who's a
    Good boy then?' This shows a

Lack of knowledge of the boozer-
Keeper's dog. It is a bruiser,
    Not a dreamy dozer.

Up it sprang and ate de Souza,
The American composer.
He is dead, the dog-enthuser.

DON'T POKE DOGS OUTSIDE THE BOOZER.
YOU ARE BOUND TO BE THE LOSER.

Kit Wright

Bengal

There once was a man of Bengal
Who was asked to a fancy dress ball;
    He murmured: 'I'll risk it
    and go as a biscuit . . .'
But a dog ate him up in the hall.

Piano Practice

A doting father once there was
Who loved his daughter Gerda,
Until she got the piano craze—
Then how the passion stirred her!
Her fingers were wild elephants' feet,
And as month after month he heard her
He tried every way
To stop her play
From bribery to murder.

One day when she was practising
He popped up behind and caught her
And dumped her in his wheelbarrow
And carried her off to slaughter.
Tipping her into a well, he cried,
'Hurrah! I've drowned my daughter!'
But a voice from the well
Rang out like a bell,
'Aha – there isn't any water!'

Ian Serraillier

Susie Had a Baby

Susie had a baby
She called him Tiny Tim
She put him in the bathtub
To see if he could swim
He drank up all the water
He ate up all the soap
He tried to eat the bathtub
But it wouldn't go down his throat.
Susie called the doctor
Susie called the nurse
Susie called the lady with the alligator purse.
Mumps said the doctor
Measles said the nurse
Chickenpox said the lady with the alligator purse.
Out went the doctor
Out went the nurse
Out went the lady with the alligator purse.

Traditional rhyme

Little William

Little William without a doubt
Pulled his baby's eyeballs out.
Jumped on them to make them pop,
Daddy said, 'Now William, stop.'

P. Gale

Careless Willie

Willie, with a thirst for gore,
Nailed his sister to the door.
Mother said, with humour quaint:
'Willie dear, don't scratch the paint.'

Night-starvation
or
The Biter Bit

At night, my Uncle Rufus
(Or so I've heard it said)
Would put his teeth into a glass
Of water by his bed.

At three o'clock one morning
He woke up with a cough,
And as he reached out for his teeth—
They bit his hand right off.

Carey Blyton

Little Dick

Little Dick,
He was so quick,
He tumbled over the timber,
He bent his bow,
To shoot a crow,
And shot the cat in the winder.

Traditional American rhyme

Lord Gorbals

Once, as old Lord Gorbals motored
  Round his moors near John O'Groats,
He collided with a goatherd
  And a herd of forty goats.
By the time his car got through
They were all defunct but two.

Roughly he addressed the goatherd:
  'Dash my whiskers and my corns!
Can't you teach your goats, you dotard,
  That they ought to sound their horns?

Look, my A.A. badge is bent!
I've a mind to raise your rent!'

Harry Graham

Exploding Albertt

Exploding Albertt
came into the room.
Boom, boom, boom,
BOOM! BOOM! BOOM!
He munched on a grape
and licked a meringue,
Bang, bang, bang,
BANG! BANG! BINGUE!
On the third of the month
and every wet Friday
Albertt exploded,
but he was neat and tidy.
'Oh dear and oh gosh,'
he'd exclaim with a blush.
'I've gone all to pieces,
please pass me a brush.'
He'd sweep himself up
and replace every bit;
he'd stick them on tight
to make sure that they'd fit.

Our Albertt was puzzled,
he scratched at his head.
'Why can't I explode
on a Thursday instead?
Or the fourth of the month,
or when it's not raining?'
No one could tell him,
there seemed no explaining.
Boom, boom went our Albertt,
boom, boom and crash wallop,
his limbs flew in the air
and came down in a dollop.

He exploded so much
(Oh much more than before!)
he blew off the roof,
one window and a door.
'I'm shocked, I'm amazed,'
said his auntie called Hortense.
'This time it's too much,
you should really have more sense.'
Albertt checked in his diary,
(he was playing a hunch),
it was wet. It was Friday,
AND the third of the month.
'That explains it,'
boomed Albertt.

Peter Mortimer

One Afternoon

I shouted to a man at the end of the pier,
'Look out, mister, don't go too near.'
For the tide was in, and the water deep,
And people in their deck-chairs were fast asleep,
With hardly a seagull hovering in the sky
To see a man who was about to die.
I ran as fast as I could to where
He was swaying and muttering in watery air,
I said to him as loud as I could,
'Don't lean on the rail, don't step on the wood,
For the planks are rotten, and the iron is thin,
And I wouldn't like to see you falling in.'
But he stuck out his tongue, made a face at me,
And then with a laugh jumped into the sea
With his umbrella and bowler hat,
And didn't come up, so that was that.

And the people dozed on, and had their dreams
Of candyfloss and soft ice-creams.

Leonard Clark

The Story of Flying Robert

When the rain comes tumbling down
In the country or the town,
All good little girls and boys
Stay at home and mind their toys.
Robert thought, 'No, when it pours,
It is better out of doors.'
Rain it did, and in a minute
Bob was in it.
Here you see him, silly fellow,
Underneath his red umbrella.

What a wind! oh! how it whistles
Through the trees and flowers and thistles!
It has caught his red umbrella:
Now look at him, silly fellow—
Up he flies
To the skies.
No one heard his screams and cries;
Through the clouds the rude wind bore him,
And his hat flew on before him.

Soon they got to such a height,
They were nearly out of sight.
And the hat went up so high,
That it nearly touched the sky.
No one ever yet could tell
Where they stopped, or where they fell:
Only this one thing is plain,
Bob was never seen again!

Heinrich Hoffman

Julius Caesar

Julius Caesar, the Roman geezer,
Squashed his wife with a lemon squeezer.

Children's playground rhyme

Algy Met a Bear

Algy met a bear,
The bear met Algy,
The bear was bulgy,
The bulge was Algy.

The Pig

The pig exclaimed, on seeing the slicer,
'I think this world might well be nicer—

Which of us, should a vote be taken,
Would want to finish up as bacon?'

The slicer rasped, 'Now listen, pig!
Your brains are small; your bottom's big.

This world is full of woe and waste—
Be grateful you're to someone's taste!'

Edward Lucie Smith

There Is a Happy Land

There is a happy land, far far away,
Where little piggies run, three times a day.
Oh! how they squeal and run
When they hear the butcher come,
Three slices off their bum, three times a day.

Playground song

The Fox Rhyme

Aunt was on the garden seat
    Enjoying a wee nap and
Along came a fox! teeth
    Closed with a snap and
He's running to the woods with her
    A-dangle and a-flap and—
Run, uncle, run
    And see what has happened!

Ian Serraillier

Bessie Met a Bus

Bessie met a bus,
The bus met Bessie,
The bus was messy,
The mess was Bessy.

Ruthless Rhyme

Auntie, did you feel no pain
    Falling from that apple-tree?
Will you do it, please, again?
    'Cos my friend here didn't see.

Harry Graham

Carelessness

A window-cleaner in our street
Who fell (five storeys) at my feet
Impaled himself on my umbrella.
I said: 'Come, come, you careless fella!
If my umbrella had been shut
You might have landed on my nut.'

Harry Graham

Hubroil's Strategic Error

He swallowed the pill
and then felt quite ill.
He should really have read
the label which said:
'All things may follow
if these pills you swallow.
The results will be
most alarming to see.'
And alarming they were,
Hubroil smelt like a sewer.
He grew fat as a toad,
then as long as a road, he grew a nose big and hairy,
then wide wings like a fairy.
His skin turned bright blue,
his mouth said 'moo, moo!'
He flew up in the air,
and then growled like a bear.
His hair went corroded
then both legs exploded.
His arms floated away.
His head went the same way!
He bounced off the ground,
and went quite green and round,
until soon he was looking
like an apple for cooking.
'That'll do for me pie,'
said a dame who passed by.
And with no further thought,
poor Hubroil was caught.
Sliced up in a pot
and cooked (o so hot).
He's under the pastry
for acting so hasty.

Peter Mortimer

Nasty MacGhastly

Nasty MacGhastly, who lives down our road,
Keeps worms in his pockets, or so I've been told.
He's always so filthy that it comes as no shock
To hear that a snake made a home in his sock.

Nasty MacGhastly has sometimes been seen,
Covered in pond weed, all slimy and green.
His parents get angry, the neighbours complain,
But Nasty just laughs and dives down a drain.

Nasty MacGhastly once ate a mouse.
His mother turned purple and fled from the house.
Left on his own Nasty didn't much care
He followed the mouse with a chocolate eclair.

Nasty MacGhastly, people now say,
Has been too much trouble and must go away.
They baited a trap with some worms and a bat
And Nasty MacGhastly was caught like a rat.

Let this be a lesson to all little boys
Who prefer creepy crawlies to playing with toys,
There's a cage with your name on, waiting for you
Next door to MacGhastly's, down at the zoo.

Charles Davies

Three Bad Ones

Tom tied a kettle to the tail of a cat,
Jill put a stone in the blind man's hat,
Bob threw his grandmother down the stairs—
And they all grew up ugly, and nobody cares.

Nursery rhyme

Don't Care

Don't Care didn't care,
Don't Care was wild:
Don't Care stole plum and pear
Like any beggar's child.

Don't Care was made to care,
Don't Care was hung:
Don't Care was put in a pot
And boiled till he was done.

Traditional

Billy the Kid

Billy was a bad man
And carried a big gun,
He was always chasing women
And kept 'em on the run.

He shot men every morning
Just to make a morning meal—
If his gun ran out of bullets
He killed them with cold steel.

He kept folks in hot water,
And he stole from many a stage,
When his gut was full of liquor
He was always in a rage.

But one day he met a man
Who was a whole lot badder—
And now he's dead—
And we ain't none the sadder.

Anon.

I Wish I Were a Bobby

I wish I were a Bobby,
Dressed up in Bobby's clothes,
With a big tall hat,
And a belly full of fat,
And a pancake in front for a nose.

I saw one on the corner
Eating Christmas pie,
I asked him for a skinny bit,
He hit me in the eye.

I went and told my mother,
My mother wouldn't come,
So I went and got the rolling pin,
And bashed him on the bum.

Two Tom Cats

Not last night but the night before,
Two tom cats came knocking at my door;
I went downstairs to let them in,
They knocked me down with a rolling pin.
The rolling pin was made of brass,
They turned me up and smacked my arse.

Children's playground rhymes

The Spider

I'm an acrobat.
I climb the air,
Out of myself spinning
The frail thread of my stair.

I build a round house, a house of silk.
It is a glittering diamond snare
When the morning sun quivers upon
Dewdrops hanging there.

I'm an ogre. I sit in a corner and wait.
Someone comes blundering by
And in my silk is ensnared—
A helpless, goggling fly.

More and more come.
My larder is full of meat.
On my spindly legs I run out
And I eat and I eat and I eat.

Olive Dove

The Scorpion

The Scorpion is as black as soot,
He dearly loves to bite;
He is a most unpleasant brute
To find in bed at night.

Hilaire Belloc

A Bug Sat in a Silver Flower

A bug sat in a silver flower
Thinking silver thoughts.
A bigger bug out for a walk
Climbed up that silver flower stalk
And snapped the small bug down his jaws
Without a pause
Without a care
For all the bug's small silver thoughts.
It isn't right
It isn't fair
That big bug ate that little bug
Because that little bug was there.

He also ate his underwear.

Karla Kuskin

Bug in a Jug

Curious fly,
Vinegar jug,
Slippery edge,
Pickled bug.

A Bug and a Flea

A bug and a flea went out to sea
Upon a reel of cotton;
The flea was drowned but the bug was found
Biting a lady's bottom.

Children's playground rhyme

Insults

Questions, Quistions and Quoshtions

Daddy how does an elephant feel
When he swallows a piece of steel?
Does he get drunk
And fall on his trunk
Or roll down the road like a wheel?

Daddy what would a pelican do
If he swallowed a bottle of glue?
Would his beak get stuck
Would he run out of luck
And lose his job at the zoo?

Son tell me tell me true,
If I belted you with a shoe,
Would you fall down dead?
Would you go up to bed?
— Either of those would do.

Spike Milligan

Roses Are Red

Roses are red, violets are blue,
Onions stink, and so do you.

Roses are red, cabbages are green,
My face may be funny, but yours is a scream.

Autograph verses

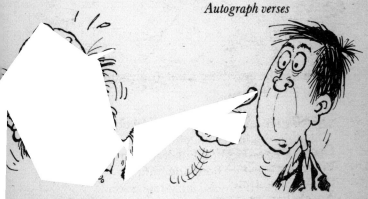

Some People

Some people
are always passing comments.
They say to me:
hallo hairy
your hands are huge
do you know your eyes pop out?
you're a monster
you aren't half white
your fingers are like sausages
you walk like a bear
is that thing on your chin a wart?

Michael Rosen

Oh Honey!

Oh honey, you're a funny 'un,
With a face like a pickled onion,
A nose like a squashed tomato,
And teeth like green peas.

Autograph verse

Horrible Things

'What's the horriblest thing you've seen?'
Said Nell to Jean.

'Some grey-coloured, trodden-on plasticine;
On a plate, a left-over cold baked bean;
A cloak-room ticket numbered thirteen;
A slice of meat without any lean;
The smile of a spiteful fairy-tale queen;
A thing in the sea like a brown submarine;
A cheese fur-coated in brilliant green;
A bluebottle perched on a piece of sardine.
What's the horriblest thing *you've* seen?'
Said Jean to Nell.

'Your face, as you tell
Of all the horriblest things you've seen.'

Roy Fuller

Grow Up

Grow up, grow up.
Every time I look at you
I throw up.

Autograph verse

Cry Baby

Cry baby, cry,
Punch him in the eye
Hang him on the lamppost
And leave him there to dry.

A Pinch and a Punch

A pinch and a punch
For the first of the month,
And no returns.

A pinch and a kick
For being so quick.

A slap in the eye
For being so sly.

A pinch and a blow
For being so slow.

Now don't be so fast
Because I'm the last
– to punch you!

Children's playground game

Tell-tale Tit

Tell-tale tit,
Your tongue shall be slit,
And all the doggies in the town
Shall have a little bit.

Children's playground rhyme

Blue Eyes, Snooty

Blue eyes, snooty,
Do your mother's duty;
Brown eyes, pinch a pie,
Run away and tell a lie;
Grey eyes, greedy gut,
Gobble all the wide world up.

Children's playground rhyme

I Hate Harry

I hate Harry like . . . like . . . OOO!
I hate Harry like . . . GEE!
I hate that Harry like – poison.
I hate! hate! hate! HAR-RY!

Rat! Dope! Skunk! Bum! Liar!
Dumber than the dumbest dumb flea!
BOY! . . . do I hate Harry,
I hate him the most that can be.

I hate him a hundred, thousand, million
Doubled, and multiplied by three,
A skillion, trillion, zillion more times
Than Harry, that rat, hates me.

Miriam Chaikin

There She Goes

There she goes, there she goes,
Piddly heels and pointed toes,
Look at her feet,
She thinks she's neat,
Long black stockings and dirty feet.

Children's playground rhyme

Christopher Robin

Hush, hush,
Nobody cares!
Christopher Robin
Has
   Fallen
     Down-
       Stairs.

J. B. Morton

Your Brother Danny

Your brother Danny's got a golden nose
and fish swim out of his eyes.
Your brother Danny's got legs like rhubarb
and ears like apple pies.

Michael Rosen

Here Comes the Bride

Here comes the bride,
Sixty inches wide,
See how she wobbles,
From side to side.

Children's playground song

Index of titles

Index of first lines

Acknowledgements

The authors and publishers would like to thank the following people for giving permission to include in this anthology material which is their copyright. The publishers have made every effort to trace the copyright holders. If we have inadvertently omitted to acknowledge anyone we should be most grateful if this could be brought to our attention for correction at the first opportunity.

George Allen & Unwin Limited for 'The Centipede's Song' by Roald Dahl from *James and the Giant Peach*

Edward Arnold Limited for 'Auntie, Did You Feel No Pain?', 'Carelessness', 'Impetuous Samuel', 'Lord Gorbals', 'Quiet Fun', and 'There's Been an Accident' by Harry Graham from *Ruthless Rhymes* and *More Ruthless Rhymes*

Beatrice D. Bartlett for 'The Spider' by Olive Dove, broadcast on BBC Radio's *Poetry Corner*

Robert Clark and Hodder & Stoughton Children's Books for 'One Afternoon' by Leonard Clark

William Cole for 'Two Sad', and 'The Slithergadee' by Shel Silverstein

Charles Davies for 'Nasty McGhastly'

Dobson Books Limited for 'Crocodile or Alligator?' and 'The Melancholy Cannibal' by Colin West from *Back to Front and Back Again*

Gerald Duckworth & Company Limited for 'Henry King' and 'The Scorpion' by Hilaire Belloc from *The Complete Verse of Hilaire Belloc*

Faber and Faber Limited for 'Night Starvation' from *Bananas in Pyjamas* by Carey Blyton

Fontana Paperbacks for 'Snoozing By the Boozer' by Kit Wright from *Rabbiting On*

A. D. Peters & Company Limited for 'Christopher Robin' by J. B. Morton and 'Notting Hill Polka' by W. Bridges-Adams from *To Charlotte While Shaving* published by Barrie Books

The Poetry Society for 'Little William' by P. Gale from *Poets in School*

Punch for 'I Had a Hippopotamus' by Patrick Barrington

Routledge & Kegan Paul Limited for 'God Bless' by Peter Tinsley from *Poems for Children* edited by Michael Baldwin, and 'The Knee on its Own' by Christian Morgenstern, translated by R. F. C. Hull from *Homo Ludens* by J. Huizinga

Ian Serraillier for 'The Fox Rhyme' and 'Piano Practice'

The Society of Authors as the literary representative of the Estate of A. E. Housman, and Jonathan Cape Limited, publishers of A. E. Housman's *Collected Poems* for 'Amelia' and 'Hallelujah'

Harvey Unna and Stephen Durbridge Limited for 'Mother Knows Best' by R. C. Scriven

More Beaver Books

We hope you have enjoyed this Beaver Book. Here are some of the other poetry collections published by Beaver Books:

The Beaver Book of Skool Verse A Beaver original. An amazing collection of poems and verses about school, including playground rhymes and games, mnemonics, verses about school dinners, lessons, teachers, end of term and exams. Lots of the material came from children all over the country who sent in their favourite rhymes, and the collection was put together by Jennifer Curry, with cartoons by Graham Thompson

Poems For Fun A Beaver original. An ideal introduction to verse for younger readers, packed with poems about all kinds of fun – games, parties, puzzles, even school. Compiled by Zenka and Ian Woodward and illustrated throughout by Tony Escott

The Beaver Book of Animal Verse A Beaver original. A beautiful collection of poetry about all kinds of animals, compiled by Raymond Wilson, with superb line drawings by Tessa Barwick

These and many other Beavers are available from your local bookshop or newsagent, or can be ordered direct from: Hamlyn Paperback Cash Sales, PO Box 11, Falmouth, Cornwall TR10 9EN. Send a cheque or postal order made payable to the Hamlyn Publishing Group, for the price of the book plus postage at the following rates:
UK: 45p for the first book, 20p for the second book and 14p for each additional book ordered to a maximum charge of £1.63;
BFPO and Eire: 45p for the first book, 20p for the second book, plus 14p per copy for the next 7 books and thereafter 8p per book;
OVERSEAS: 75p for the first book and 21p for each extra book.

New Beavers are published every month and if you would like the *Beaver Bulletin*, a newsletter which tells you about new books and gives a complete list of titles and prices, send a large stamped addressed envelope to:

Beaver Bulletin
The Hamlyn Group
Astronaut House
Feltham
Middlesex TW14 9AR

20670X